# Read me a Story

# Bedtime Tales

hinkler

Published by Hinkler Books Pty Ltd
45–55 Fairchild Street
Heatherton Victoria 3202 Australia
www.hinkler.com.au

hinkler

Cover Design: 38a The Shop
Cover Illustration: Laura Watkins
Prepress: Graphic Print Group

ISBN: 978 1 7435 2923 2

Printed and bound in China

# Contents

Brown Paper Bear ...................................4

The Midnight Unicorn...................... 38

Shh! Don't Wake the Baby!................ 72

Fox Makes Friends......................... 104

Little Rabbit ................................ 136

Snow Bear .................................... 166

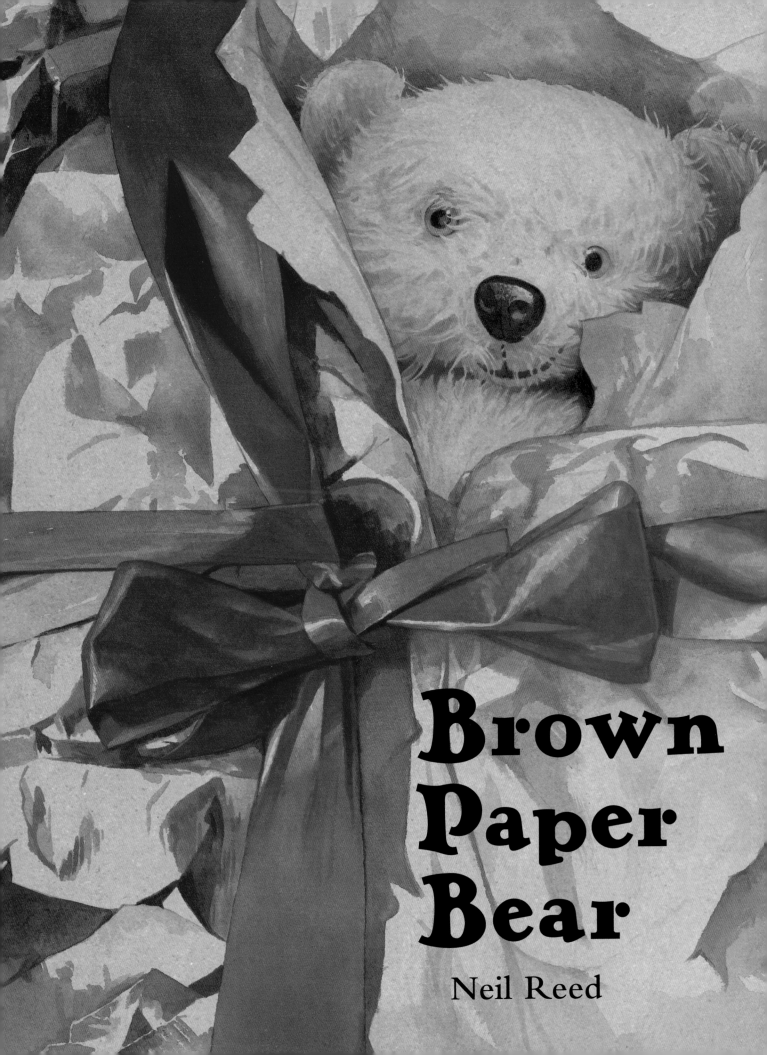

# Brown Paper Bear

### Neil Reed

# Brown
# Paper Bear

By Catherine Allison
Illustrated by Neil Reed

One dark winter's night, a magical
light entered Jessica's bedroom.

Jessica woke up and noticed a strange chest of toys in her room. The doors were wide open and seemed to be calling to her.

Inside the old toy chest there was
a collection of dusty old things: a train with
a bell, three blocks, a drum, two books, an old hat,
a cool old car, a racket and ball, and a teddy bear
wrapped in a brown paper package tied with a red ribbon.

14

Jessica unwrapped the teddy bear and held him close to her. The teddy bear's eyes opened.

15

The teddy bear had come to life! He climbed up on the little stool. "Take my hand and I will bring you to meet my friends," said the teddy bear.

Jessica took the teddy bear's hand
and magically they flew out of Jessica's
bedroom window and into the night sky.

They landed in a beautiful
playroom filled with
old-fashioned toys.
"Here are my friends," the
teddy bear said. "Wake up,
everyone!" he cried. "Meet
my new friend, Jessica."

The jack-in-the-box jumped up and
down and said, "Hello, young lady."
"Nice to meet you," said
Jessica as she giggled.

Next she stood in line with some toy soldiers.
"One, two, three, four!" shouted the head soldier.
Together she and the soldiers marched around
the playroom.

She stopped to take a ride on the toy train.
She put on the conductor's cap and sat on the
engine. The train started to move and Jessica
waved good-bye to the soldier.

Suddenly, a pull-the-string puppy jumped on top of Jessica and gave her a wet kiss. She tickled the puppy's belly and the puppy licked Jessica again.

29

The beautiful doll called to Jessica, "Come dance with me!" Together the doll and Jessica spun around the room.

"This is so much fun!" said Jessica.

The toy monkey tried to get Jessica's attention. He swung upside down and did his monkey tricks until Jessica ran after him.

33

"It's time to go," said the teddy bear. Jessica took the teddy bear's hand and said good-bye to her new friends.

"I will not forget you," she said as she flew away with the teddy bear.

35

The next morning the toy chest was gone. Jessica told her grandfather about her journey with the teddy bear in the brown paper package.

"I see you found my teddy bear," he said. The teddy bear smiled and winked.

# The Midnight Unicorn

Neil Reed

# The
# Midnight Unicorn

Illustrated
by
Neil Reed

"Where shall we go this afternoon, Millie?" said Dad, as he put on his coat.
Millie jumped up, scattering her model-making tools. There was only one place she wanted to go, at any time of year! Dad laughed and took Casper's lead from the peg by the door.

43

44

"Why do you love the park so much, Millie?"
Dad asked. "The statue is nice enough, but I
don't think it's that special. But then I stopped
believing in unicorns long ago."
Millie couldn't really explain it, but the park, and
especially that one statue, were the most important
things in the world to her.

The park was deserted. Dad and Millie took their usual path, across the playing fields, past the children's playground, and on towards the statue.

46

And there was the statue – a small, grey unicorn, mottled with age and weather, and slightly mossy around the hooves. It had the kindest, wisest smile that Millie could imagine, and she was always happy when she was nearby.

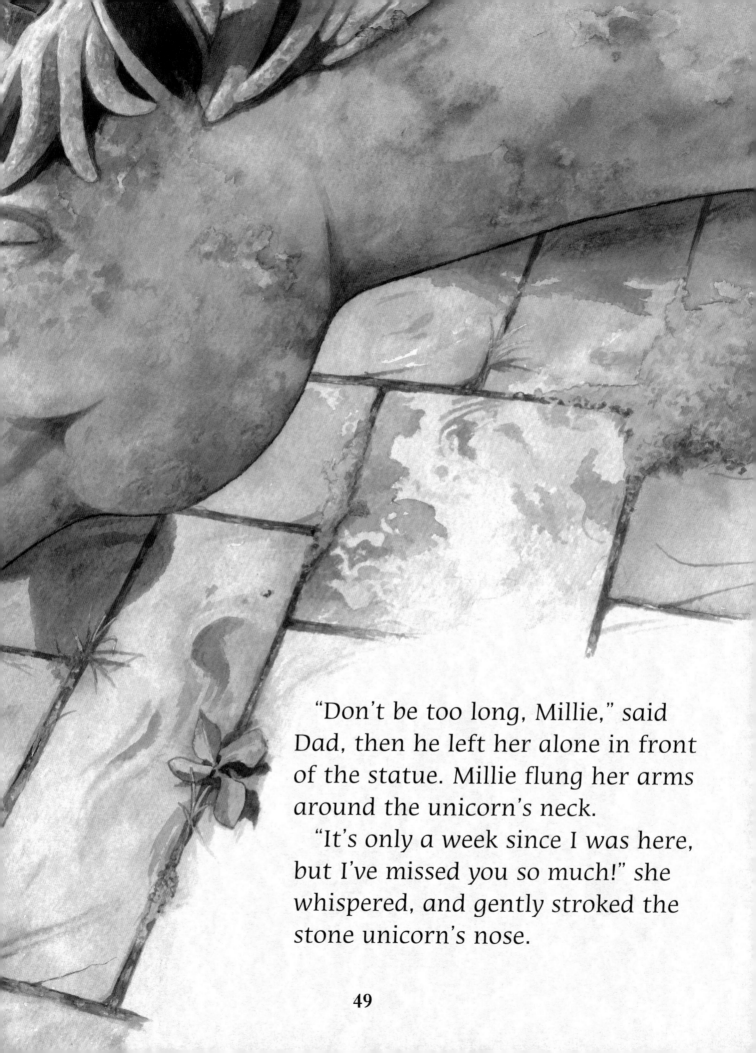

"Don't be too long, Millie," said Dad, then he left her alone in front of the statue. Millie flung her arms around the unicorn's neck.

"It's only a week since I was here, but I've missed you so much!" she whispered, and gently stroked the stone unicorn's nose.

49

50

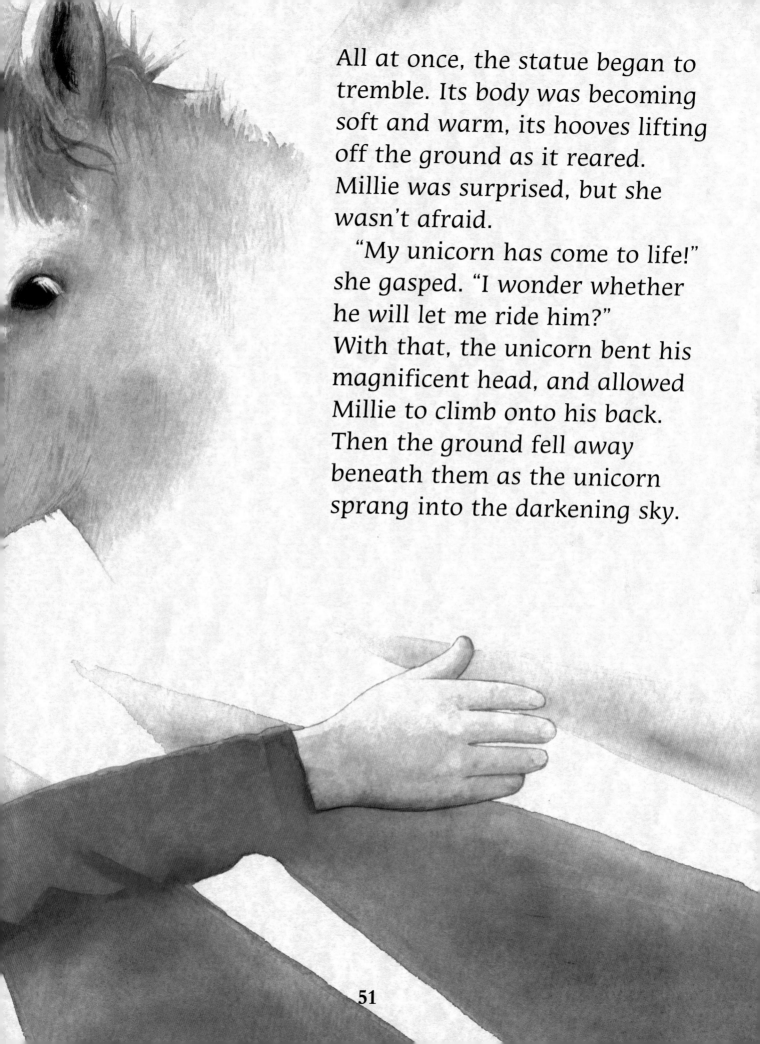

All at once, the statue began to tremble. Its body was becoming soft and warm, its hooves lifting off the ground as it reared. Millie was surprised, but she wasn't afraid.

"My unicorn has come to life!" she gasped. "I wonder whether he will let me ride him?" With that, the unicorn bent his magnificent head, and allowed Millie to climb onto his back. Then the ground fell away beneath them as the unicorn sprang into the darkening sky.

51

Up and up they flew, high over the town. At first Millie was so scared that she could hardly open her eyes, but soon she got used to the speed and the rushing wind. The ground was far below, and the sky around her was full of stars.

"What a wonderful ride!" she cried out in delight.

Casper didn't feel as comfortable in the air!

The town clock struck midnight.

Millie and the unicorn flew on, over hills and forests and lakes. Then the wind came up again.

"There's a storm coming," Millie called out. "We'll have to fly fast to beat it. Hold on tight, Casper!"

The unicorn put his head down and charged through the angry clouds. Lightning crashed, and rain beat into Millie's face. Casper flew close beside them, whimpering now and then as the thunder boomed.

At last, the storm cleared.

Millie looked up, and gasped at what she saw. The unicorn was flying over glistening icy mountains, the peaks flashing like needles in the sun. Casper barked excitedly.

"Wow!" said Millie. "Can we fly closer?"

With that, the unicorn swooped so low that Millie could run her fingers through the snow.

The air was full of icy spray
as they dived, and Millie was so
excited she could hardly breathe!

57

"That was brilliant!"
cried Millie, "but I'm
cold now. Let's go somewhere
warmer." The unicorn wheeled
and in no time at all they were
gliding through the warm desert
night, surrounded by stars, with
red sand dunes stretching out
far below them.

"Now take me somewhere really exciting,
Unicorn!" shouted Millie. So the unicorn
turned out over a sparkling opal sea. Waves
rolled and crashed on to a distant beach,
and as Millie looked, she began to make out
other unicorns, prancing in the foam.
To her delight, the unicorn spiralled down, down,
right into the breakers, to join them in their fun.
The glittering spray soaked her to the skin, but she
just giggled!

61

With the pounding waves still ringing in her
ears, Millie pulled gently on the unicorn's
mane. The unicorn climbed easily into the
air and set off to ride a rainbow far out
to sea. Millie could see that the rainbow
was leading them to a beautiful island,
all alone in the dark sea, lit by a shaft
of golden daylight. And as they got
closer and closer, Millie saw that
the island was full of unicorns!

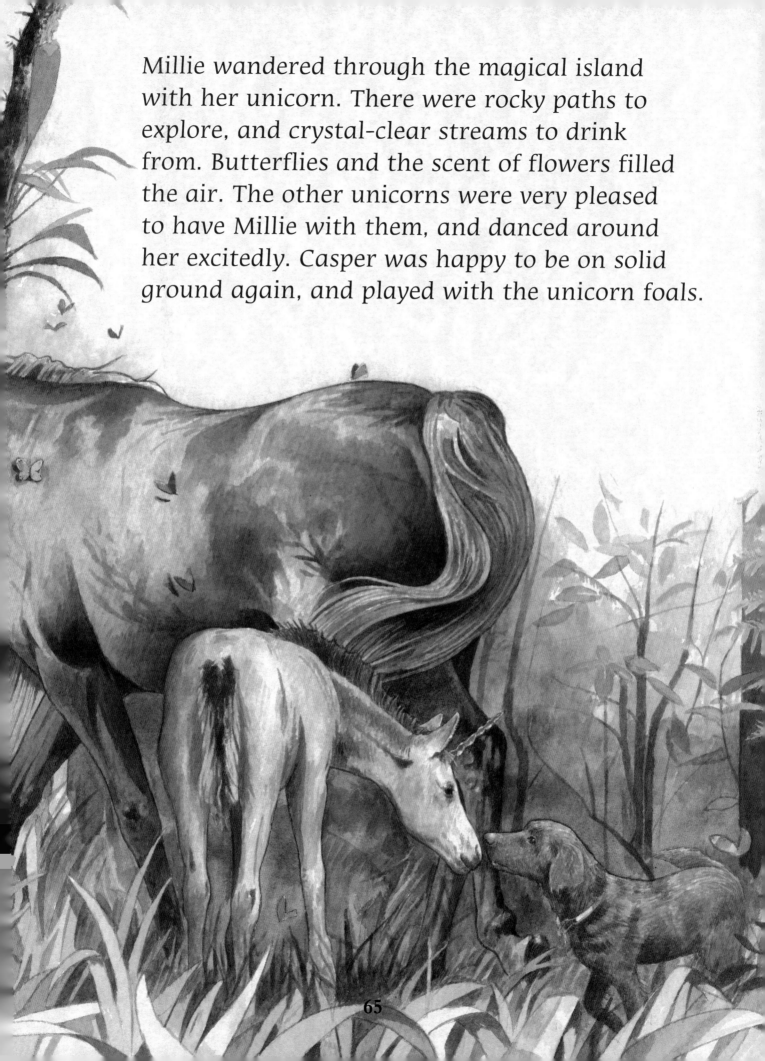

Millie wandered through the magical island
with her unicorn. There were rocky paths to
explore, and crystal-clear streams to drink
from. Butterflies and the scent of flowers filled
the air. The other unicorns were very pleased
to have Millie with them, and danced around
her excitedly. Casper was happy to be on solid
ground again, and played with the unicorn foals.

At last, exhausted by all their adventures, the girl, her dog and her unicorn lay down on the sweet grass. Butterfly wings fanned them gently into a deep, calm sleep.

"Millie?" called Dad. "Millie, it's time to go now."
Millie awoke to find herself hugging the cold stone head
of the statue.
"Dad, I've had the best adventure! The unicorn came to
life and we flew off around the world. I saw the most
amazing places!"
"You have such a wonderful imagination, Millie," laughed
Dad, shaking his head.
"No, Dad. That's the most amazing part. In my dream, I
could really see. I wasn't blind."

For a moment, Millie
wondered how much to
tell her dad. But then she
stopped. It was her secret,
hers and the unicorn's.
    "I know it's true," she said to
herself, and leant forward
to kiss the unicorn.

"Thank you, my midnight
unicorn," she whispered. Then
Dad led her back to the path,
out through the park gates,
and home.

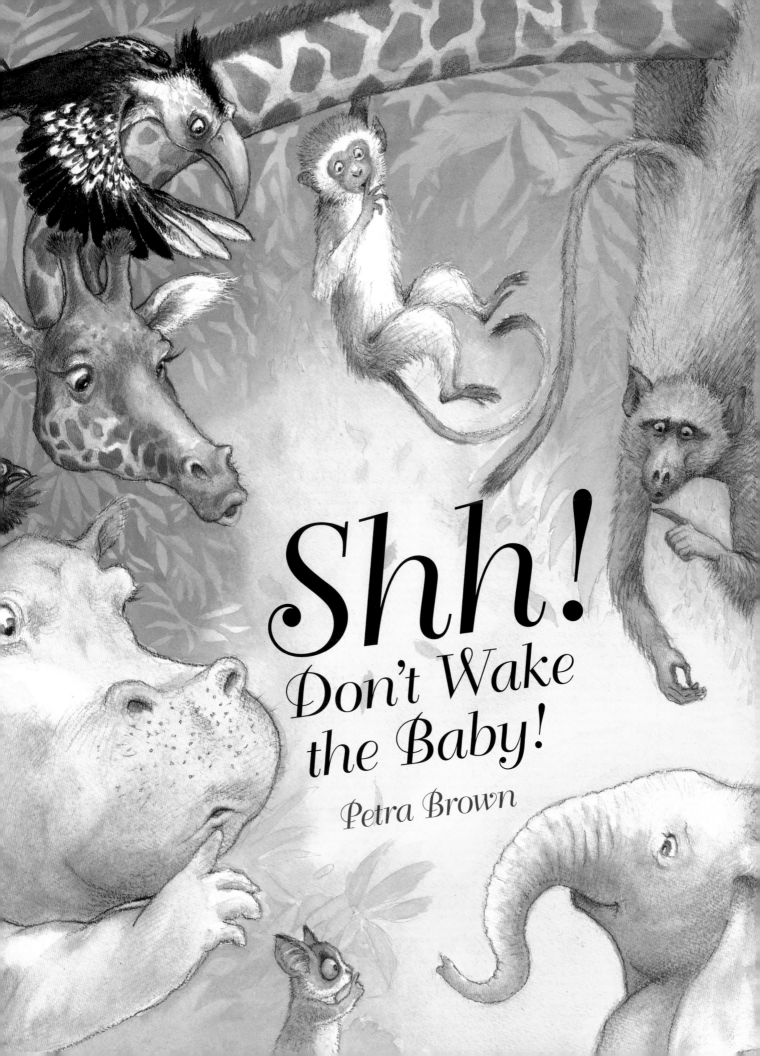

# Shh!
## Don't Wake the Baby!

Petra Brown

# Shh!
## Don't Wake the Baby!

Petra Brown

In amongst the shady trees, and close by the waterhole, Mummy Elephant had just got her new baby off to sleep.

"Now, Little Elephant," she said to her son, "Please be very quiet this afternoon, so that you don't wake the baby."

Little Elephant loved his mummy, and wanted to be good.

"OK, Mummy. I'll be quiet!" he said, and he gave her a big kiss, and ran off to find something quiet to do.

Little Elephant wasn't known for being quiet. He could make a big hullabaloo doing even the smallest thing! So he crashed through the forest, trampled down the undergrowth, and generally made an awful, joyful din.

Giraffe stretched down her long neck and said, "Shh! Don't wake the baby!"

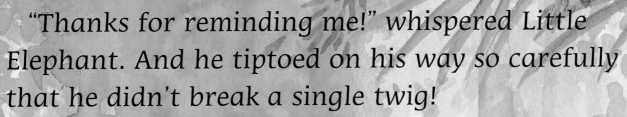

"Thanks for reminding me!" whispered Little
Elephant. And he tiptoed on his way so carefully
that he didn't break a single twig!

"That's better!" said Giraffe kindly, and went back
to her lunch. The forest was quiet once more.

Of all his favourite things to do, bathing in the waterhole was Little Elephant's best. So at the water's edge, he didn't stop to think, he just dived in with a huge...

SPLASH!

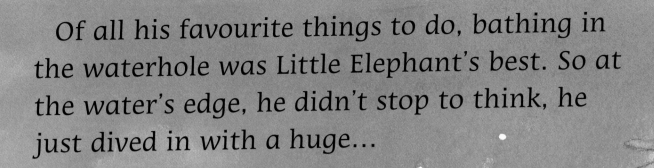

Then he noisily sucked up a trunkful of cool muddy water, and poured it over his head. What bliss!

84

But Hippo, amongst others,
was not impressed.
"Shh! Don't wake the baby!" she glared at him.

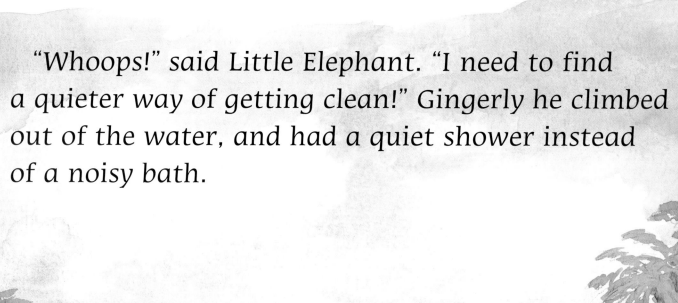

"Whoops!" said Little Elephant. "I need to find a quieter way of getting clean!" Gingerly he climbed out of the water, and had a quiet shower instead of a noisy bath.

Once he was clean, Little Elephant was ravenous! So he rushed to his favourite tree, and took a huge trunkful of sweet juicy leaves.

"Yum!" he slurped, and pulled down another branch, making the whole tree shake and shudder. He had no idea that he was making a big noise, but he *was*! Grandpa Vervet scowled and hissed at him, "Ssh! You'll wake that baby, you know!"

"I'm just eating like everyone else!" pleaded Little Elephant.

"But you're bigger and messier and noisier than everyone else," said the monkey crossly. Then, seeing that Little Elephant was truly upset, he and the other monkeys showed him how to eat more quietly.

Little Elephant was miserable. He couldn't do any of his favourite things without being noisy. And he'd never had so many tellings off in one day!

He gave a big sigh,
and settled down
to consider how
unfair it all was.

All of a sudden, he got a funny feeling in his trunk. It was a bit like a tickle… or was it more of a snuffle? Little Elephant blinked and shook his tickly trunk from side to side.

"Something's going to happen," he thought, "and it isn't going to be quiet!" He gave a gasping, helpless snort and...

# ATCHOO!!!

"YOU'VE WOKEN THE BABY!!"
*groaned Mummy Elephant.*

Flowers and leaves fluttered down around them. One flower landed in Baby's cradle. All the animals held their breath, waiting for her to scream...

99

...but Baby just giggled!
"Phew!" said Little Elephant.

101

103

# Fox Makes Friends

Adam Relf

# Fox
# Makes
# Friends

## Adam Relf

Fox sat in his room.
He was bored.
"I know," he said.
"I need a friend."

Fox picked up his net and went to see his mum.
"I'm going to catch a friend," he declared.
"You can't catch friends," Mum explained.
"You have to *make* friends."
So Fox put down his net and
set off to make a friend.

"What can I make a friend out of?"
he thought.
    He picked up some sticks, an apple
    and some nuts, and fixed them
    all together. At last he had
    a brand new friend standing
    in front of him.

"Are you my friend?" Fox asked,
but the friend said nothing.
"Can you come and play?" he said,
but the friend didn't move."Maybe he's
too small," Fox thought. "I need to make
a bigger friend!"

Just then a rabbit ran by.
"Excuse me," said Fox. "I'm trying
to make a friend but this one is
too small. Can you help me
make a bigger one?"
"Okay," said Rabbit.

They worked together and picked up a turnip, some tomatoes, and some twigs. They stuck them all together and soon they had a bigger friend standing before them.

"Will you be our friend?" they asked, but there was no answer.

"Can you come and play?" they said,
but the friend just stood there.
"Maybe he's still too small,"
said Rabbit.

A moment later Fox and Rabbit heard giggling in the treetops. It was a squirrel.
"What a mess you two are making!" he laughed.
"Well, if you can do better, come down and help us!" said Fox
"Okay," said Squirrel.

This time all three of them set to work. They picked up a huge pumpkin, a turnip, some branches and some apples. They put them all together and had the biggest friend they could make.

"Are you our friend?" they asked.

"Please can you come and play?"

But there was no reply.

Finally they all gave up.
"Oh well," said Fox. "I suppose I will never be able to make a friend."

Just then Fox's mother
came by.
"Hello," she said. "Who are
all your new friends?"
"Oh," said Fox. "My plan
didn't work. We made friends
but they won't play with us."
"Not them!" giggled his mother.
"These friends!" she said,
pointing to Squirrel
and Rabbit.

Fox looked over at Squirrel and Rabbit, and suddenly realised that he had been making friends all along!

131

So Fox, Squirrel, and Rabbit
played for the rest of the
day, and they stayed
friends forever.

134

# Little Rabbit

Piers Harper

# Little Rabbit

Illustrated by Piers Harper

Little Rabbit was the very littlest rabbit in his family. But being the littlest in a big family wasn't always much fun.

Little Rabbit liked to hop and bounce, but his bigger brothers and sisters didn't always let him join in their games. He liked to cuddle up with his mummy and daddy, but they were mostly too busy.

Sometimes Little Rabbit thought no one even remembered he was there.

So, one day, when no one was paying him any attention, he decided to go and find a new family – a family who always had time to play with him. Off he hopped, leaving his mummy, his daddy and all his brothers and sisters behind.

Little Rabbit hopped and hopped until he heard rustling and scampering noises. He peeped through some golden corn, and there was a family of field mice.

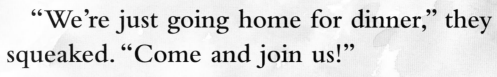

"We're just going home for dinner," they squeaked. "Come and join us!"

"Maybe this family will look after me," thought Little Rabbit, and he skipped away happily with them.

When they arrived, Mummy Mouse laid out a meal of nuts and berries for them to share.

"Help yourself, Little Rabbit," she said. Little Rabbit turned pink to the tips of his ears.

"I'm sorry," he said, "but rabbits can't eat nuts and berries." He remembered how his mummy always fetched him the sweetest grasses and dandelions to eat. "You've been very kind, but I don't think I belong in your family."

And he bounced away towards the river.

When he reached the riverbank, he saw some animals rolling and playing together. It was a family of otters. Two cubs swam up to him.

"We're playing chase," they called. "Come and join us!"

"Maybe this family will look after me," thought Little Rabbit.

But Little Rabbit soon found that he couldn't play the otters' splishy, splashy river games He didn't even like getting his feet wet. He remembered the fun he used to have playing hide-and-seek with his brothers and sisters. "I don't think I belong in this family, either," he thought.

So Little Rabbit said goodbye and bounced away towards the forest.

Soon Little Rabbit heard a tap, tap, tap in the trees and, looking up, he saw a flash of speckled feathers through the leaves. It was a family of woodpeckers.

Two chicks flew down to him.

"We're helping our daddy find food," they said. "Come and join us!"

"Maybe this family will look after me," thought Little Rabbit.

The chicks were very friendly, but
Little Rabbbit couldn't really join in.
Watching the woodpeckers with their
daddy had reminded him of how he used
to dig in the burrow with *his* daddy.
He loved doing that!

"It was nice to meet you," he said to the woodpeckers, after a while. "But I don't think I belong in your family." And he bounced away again.

157

Little Rabbit was beginning to think he'd never find a new family when he met some ponies trotting along in the sunshine. He ran to catch them up.

"Hello, Little Rabbit," the ponies said. "Why don't you run along with us for a while? It's a beautiful day!"

"What fun!" said Little Rabbit, and they set off, with the wind rushing through their fur.

But the ponies were much faster than he was, and soon Little Rabbit felt tired. He needed to rest. "Please can we stop?" he called out. But the wind was whistling so loudly that they couldn't hear him and, in a moment, they were gone.

Poor Little Rabbit was left all alone. His ears drooped.
None of the families he'd met had been right for him,
and the more he thought about his own rabbit family,
the more he realised that he missed them.

He sighed and looked across the fields. Just then, he saw some rabbits in the distance. And there, running towards him, were his mummy, his daddy, and all his brothers and sisters!

"Oh, Little Rabbit, we were so worried about you," his mummy said, when they were safely back at home. "Please don't ever run off again."

"I won't," said Little Rabbit, sleepily. "Because this is where I belong, isn't it?"

"Yes, Little Rabbit, it is," said his mummy. "And we all love you very much."

"I love you, too," said Little Rabbit, and he smiled and closed his eyes.

Piers Harper

# SNOW
# BEAR

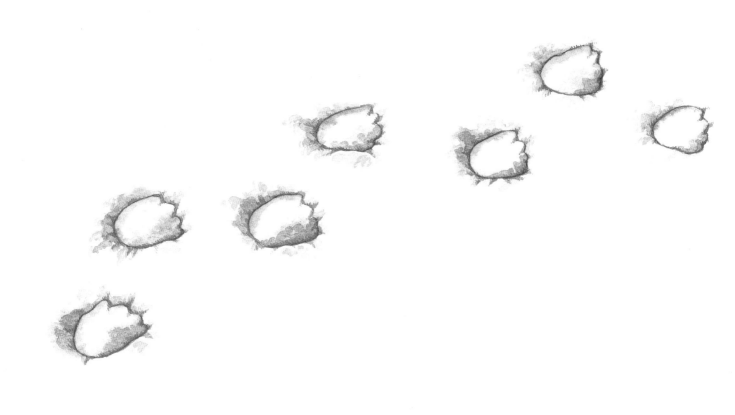

# SNOW BEAR

Piers Harper

Little Snow Bear had been snuggled up with his mother all winter inside their cosy den. He was longing to go outside.

On the first day of spring, his mother said, "It's time for you to meet the world, my little one."

Little Snow Bear rolled around in the soft, powdery snow. It was so much fun, he did it again and again!

"Now you can go and explore," said his mother. "But stay by the water's edge where I can see you. I don't want you getting lost."

Little Snow Bear ran down to the water. It was blue and shimmery—the most beautiful thing he had ever seen.

He saw something swimming in the water, making it ripple and splash. So he went to take a closer look.

"Hello," said a little seal. "Do you want to come play with me?"

The water looked so exciting that Little Snow Bear jumped right in—*SPLASH!* Exploring was so much fun!

Little Snow Bear had a great time playing splashing games with his new friend. Soon he remembered what his mother had said about getting lost. He looked around, but he did not see her anywhere. He got out of the water and shook himself dry. "Good-bye," he said to the little seal, and he set off to find his mother.

Little Snow Bear padded across the ice, but he soon found himself in a big forest. He was just starting to feel a little worried when he heard a friendly voice.

"Hello there," said a reindeer. "What are you doing here all alone?"

"I'm exploring," said Little Snow Bear. "But now I need to find my mother."

"Come with me," said the reindeer kindly.
"I'll show you the way out of the forest."

Once outside the forest, Little Snow Bear was sure his mother would be waiting ... but she was not there! Suddenly exploring was not so much fun. His tummy rumbled. He felt hungry.

Nearby, Little Snow Bear saw a little girl fishing.

"Hello," said the little girl. "What are doing out here all alone?"

"I was exploring," Little Snow Bear said, sniffling. "But now I'm hungry. I'm tired and I'm lost—and I want my mother."

"Getting lost is no fun at all,"
said the little girl. "Don't worry.
I'll help you find your mother.
But first, I will give you
something to eat."

187

After eating a delicious fish meal, Little Snow
Bear climbed into the girl's sled.

"Come on," she said to her dogs. "Let's take
this Little Snow Bear home."

And off they sped across the snow.

"There she is!" Little Snow Bear saw his mother and ran to her.

"Where have you been?" she asked. "I've been so worried about you."

"I'm sorry I got lost," said Little Snow Bear.

"I'm so happy that you're home safe," said his mother.

Little Snow Bear began to tell her all about his adventure.

His mother gave him a big hug.
"I love you, my Little Snow Bear," she
whispered as he fell fast asleep, safe in her arms.